"HELLO READING books are a perfect introduction to reading. Brief sentences full of word repetition and full-color pictures stress visual clues to help a child take the first important steps toward reading. Mastering these storybooks will build children's reading confidence and give them the enthusiasm to stand on their own in the world of words."

—Bee Cullinan
Past President of the International Reading
Association, Professor in New York University's
Early Childhood and Elementary Education Program

"Readers aren't born, they're made. Desire is planted—planted by parents who work at it."

—Jim Trelease
author of *The Read-Aloud Handbook*

"When I was a classroom reading teacher, I recognized the importance of good stories in making children understand that reading is more than just recognizing words. I saw that children who have ready access to storybooks get excited about reading. They also make noticeably greater gains in reading comprehension. The development of the HELLO READING stories grows out of this experience."

—Harriet Ziefert
M.A.T., New York University School of Education
Author, Language Arts Module,
Scholastic Early Childhood Program

For Jon

VIKING
Published by the Penguin Group
Viking Penguin, a division of Penguin Books USA Inc.,
375 Hudson Street, New York, New York 10014, U.S.A.
Penguin Books Ltd, 27 Wrights Lane, London W8 5TZ, England
Penguin Books Australia Ltd, Ringwood, Victoria, Australia
Penguin Books Canada Ltd, 2801 John Street, Markham, Ontario, Canada L3R 1B4
Penguin Books (N.Z.) Ltd, 182-190 Wairau Road, Auckland 10, New Zealand

Penguin Books Ltd, Registered Offices: Harmondsworth, Middlesex, England

First published in 1991 by Viking Penguin, a division of Penguin Books USA Inc.

1 3 5 7 9 10 8 6 4 2

Text copyright © Harriet Ziefert, 1991
Illustrations copyright © Laura Rader, 1991
All rights reserved
Library of Congress catalog card number: 90-50714
ISBN 0-670-83859-4

Printed in Singapore for Harriet Ziefert, Inc.

Goody New Shoes

Harriet Ziefert
Pictures by Laura Rader

VIKING

Penny's mom needed a rest.
"I'll take you shopping," said Penny's dad.

"Yippee!" said Penny.
"Yippee!" said P.J.

"Buckle your seat belts," said Dad.
"Then we can go."

Vroom! Vroom!
The car started.

"Here we go," said P.J.

They parked.
They walked to the barber's.

P.J. ran ahead.
He got there first

But Penny got the first haircut.

Snip! Snip!
P.J. had to wait.

P.J. wouldn't sit still.
"Stop moving around," said Daddy.
"The barber can't cut your hair."

"Now let's go to the shoe store," said Daddy.
"Goody!" said Penny. "New shoes."
"Goody new shoes," said P.J.

P.J. window-shopped.

Penny window-shopped.

"Hurry up!" said Daddy.
"Or you'll never get new shoes."

Penny and P.J. sat down.
"Who's first?" asked the man.
"I am!" said P.J.

"Okay," said the shoe-store man. "I'll measure your feet."

"What color shoes do you want?"
asked the man.
"Not brown," said P.J.

"How about blue?" asked the man.

P.J. liked the blue shoes.
"Goody!" he said. "New shoes.
Can I wear them home?"

"What color shoes do you want?"
the man asked Penny.
"I want red ones," said Penny.

Penny didn't like any red shoes.
But she liked a pair of purple ones.
"Goody new shoes!" she said.
"Can I keep them on?"

Dad paid for the new shoes.
The lady gave Penny and P.J. balloons.

"Say thank you," said Dad.
"Thank you!" they said together.

Dad tied P.J.'s balloon around his wrist.
Then he tied Penny's.

"Let's run," said P.J.
"Okay. Let's run!" said Penny.

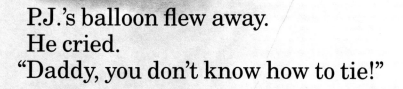

P.J.'s balloon flew away.
He cried.
"Daddy, you don't know how to tie!"

"I'm sorry," said Dad.
"I'm sorry you lost your balloon.
 But I can buy something
 you can keep for a long time."

Daddy took Penny and P.J. to a bookstore.
It was a special store—just for children.

Penny picked a book.
P.J. picked a book.

Two good books.
One for Penny.
One for P.J.
Hello Reading!